P9-DNN-753

ALL by MYSeLF!

written and illustrated by **ALIKI**

HarperCollinsPublishers

This book is for:

Peter (my inspiration)

John (his accomplished big brother)

Sam (who learned how)

Brittany (who is just doing it)

Alexa (her big sister), and

Panayiota (they know how, too)

All by Myself! • Copyright © 2000 by Aliki Brandenberg • Printed in the U.S.A. All rights reserved. • http://www.harperchildrens.com
Library of Congress Cataloging-in-Publication Data • Aliki. • All by myself! / written and illustrated by Aliki. • p.   cm.
Summary: A child shows all the things he has learned to do all on his own. • ISBN 0-06-028929-5. — ISBN 0-06-028930-9 (lib. bdg.)
[1. Self-reliance—Fiction.] I. Title. • PZ7.A397 Al   2000 • [E]—dc21 • 99-51672   CIP   AC
1 2 3 4 5 6 7 8 9 10 ❖ First Edition

Run to the bathroom,
fast as an elf.

Sit,

wash,

brush,

all by myself.

Down with the bottoms,

up with the top.

Down with the shirt,

and snap it all up.

Pull up the blue jeans,

button
and
zip.

On with the socks,

and now for a flip.

Right shoe,

left shoe.

Tie,

comb,

done!

Breakfast's ready,

pour,

crunch,

yum!

Open the
school door.

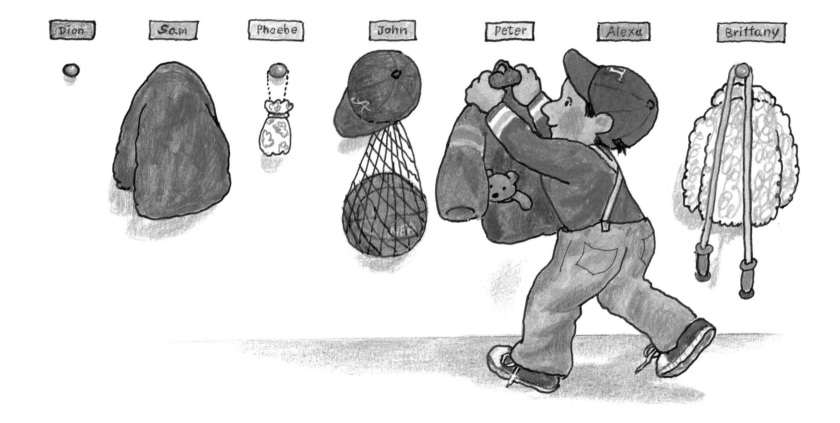

I'm on my way.

Build,

paint,

write,

sing.

Fun all day.

When school is over,

there's still more to do.

Going here,

going there.

Quiet is nice, too.

Practice my lesson.

Soon time to eat.

Help with
the dinner.

Mmm,
what a treat.

A whole day is over.

Nighttime comes.

Unsnap, up, unzip, down.

Water runs.

Steamy, dreamy,

splash, squeeze, rub.

Clean and dry now.

Good-bye, tub.

Up with the
bottoms,

down with
the top.

Choose a book.

Snuggle close.

Time to stop.

Close the light.

Say good night.

Sleep sweet dreams.

One day ends...

then another begins!

E
Alik

Aliki.

All by myself!

OCEAN COUNTY LIBRARY

JAN   2001

BAY HEAD READING CENTER
OCEAN COUNTY LIBRARY
BAY HEAD, NJ 08742   BAKER & TAYLOR